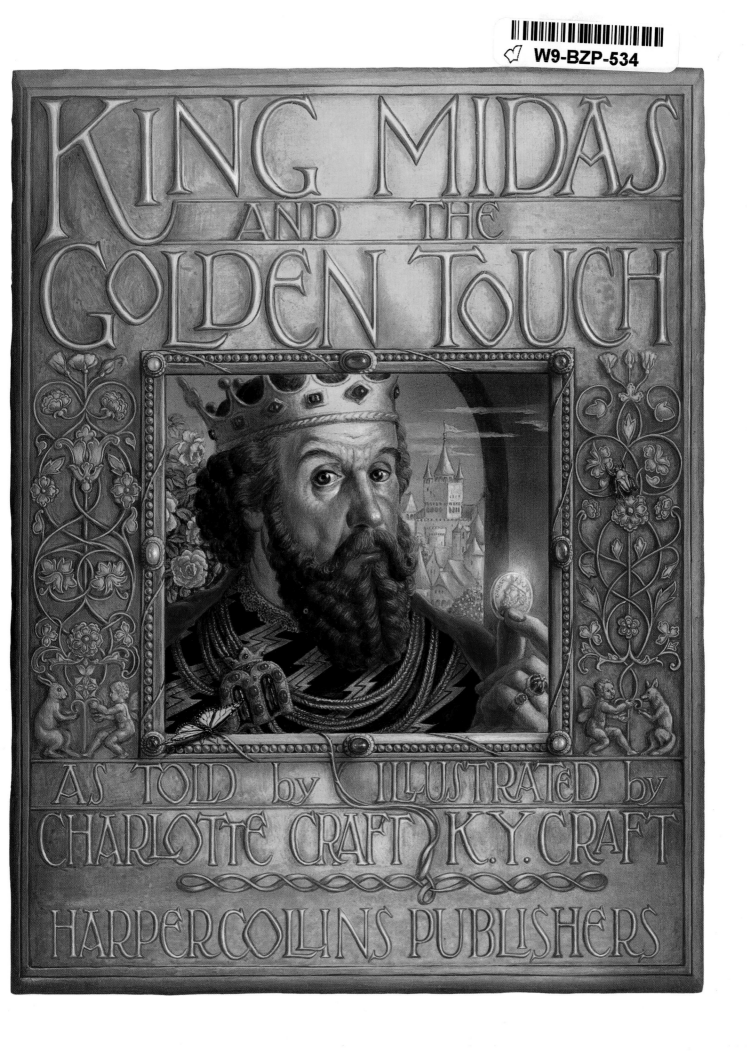

KING MIDAS
AND THE
GOLDEN TOUCH

AS TOLD by   ILLUSTRATED by
CHARLOTTE CRAFT   K.Y. CRAFT

HARPERCOLLINS PUBLISHERS

There once lived a very rich king called Midas who believed that nothing was more precious than gold. He loved its soft yellow hue and comforting weight in the palm of his hand. The chink of gold coins dropped into a leather purse sounded sweeter to him than the songs of his finest musicians. There was only one thing that Midas loved more, and that was his daughter, Aurelia.

"Aurelia," he often told her as she played by the throne, "someday I shall bequeath to you the greatest treasury of gold in all the world."

There had been a time, however, when King Midas loved roses as much as he now loved gold. He had once called together the best gardeners in his realm, and the garden they created for him became renowned for the beauty and variety of its roses.

But in time the delicate fragrances and exquisite colors meant nothing to Midas. Only Aurelia still loved the garden. Every day she would pick a bouquet of the most perfect roses to adorn the king's breakfast table. But when Midas saw the flowers, he would think, Their beauty lasts but a day. If they were gold, it would last forever!

One day the king's guards found an old man asleep under the rosebushes and brought him before King Midas.

"Unbind him," Midas ordered. "Without my gold, I would be as poor as he. Tonight he shall dine with me!"

So that night the old man sat at the king's table, where he was well fed and entertained by the king himself. And after a good night's sleep, the old man went on his way.

That morning, as he often did, Midas went down into his dungeon. With a large brass key, he unlocked the door to the secret chamber where he kept his gold. After carefully locking the door behind him, he sat down to admire his precious wealth.

"Ah, I do love it so," he sighed, gazing at his riches. "No matter how hard I work, no matter how long I live, I will never have enough."

He was lost in these thoughts when the chamber suddenly filled with light. King Midas looked up and was amazed to behold the glowing figure of a young man. Since there was no way into the room but through the locked door, Midas knew that he was in the presence of magic.

"Do you not recognize me, friend?"

Midas shook his head. The mysterious stranger smiled at him, and it seemed that all the gold in the dungeon glittered even brighter.

"I am the old man from the rose garden. Instead of punishing me for trespassing, you entertained me at your table. I had thought to reward you for your kindness, but with so much gold, you must surely want for nothing."

"That's not true," cried Midas. "A man can never have enough gold."

The stranger's smile broadened. "Well, then, what would make you a happier man?"

Midas thought for only a moment. "Perhaps if everything I touched would turn to gold," he said.

"That is your wish?"

"Yes, for then it would always be at my fingertips," Midas assured him.

"Think carefully, my friend," cautioned the visitor.

"Yes," replied Midas. "The golden touch would bring me all the happiness I need."

"And so it shall be yours."

With that, the mysterious figure became brighter and brighter, until the light became so intense that Midas had to close his eyes. When he opened them, he was alone once again.

Had the enchantment worked?

Midas eagerly rubbed the great brass door key but was greatly disappointed. There was no gold in his hands. Bewildered, he looked around the dim room and wondered if perhaps he had been dreaming.

ut when King Midas awoke the next day, he found his bedchamber bathed in golden light. Glistening in the morning sun, the plain linen bedcovers had been transformed into finely spun gold!

Jumping out of bed, he gasped with astonishment. The bedpost turned to gold as soon as he touched it. "It's true," he cried. "I have the golden touch!"

Midas pulled on his clothes. He was thrilled to find himself wearing a handsome suit of gold—never mind that it was a bit heavy. He slid his spectacles onto his nose. To his delight, they, too, turned to gold—never mind that he couldn't see through them. With a gift as great as this, he thought, no inconvenience could be too great.

Without wasting another moment, Midas rushed out of the room, through the palace, and into the garden.

The roses glistened with the morning dew, and their scent gently perfumed the air. Midas went from bush to bush, touching each of the blossoms.

"How happy Aurelia will be when she sees these roses of gold!" he exclaimed. He never noticed how the perfect golden blossoms drooped and pulled down the bushes with their weight.

Soon it was time for breakfast. Midas sat down just as Aurelia entered the room, clutching a golden rose, her face wet with tears.

"Father, Father, a horrible thing has happened," she said, sobbing. "I went to the garden to pick you a flower, but all of the roses have become hard and yellow."

"They are golden roses now, my love, and will never fade."

"But I miss their scent, Father," cried Aurelia.

"I am sorry, my dear. I thought only to please you. Now we can buy all the roses you could ever wish for." Midas smiled at his daughter to comfort her. "Please wipe your eyes, and we'll have our breakfast together."

idas lifted a spoonful of porridge to his mouth, but as soon as the porridge touched his lips it turned into a hard golden lump.

Perhaps if I eat quickly, he thought, puzzled, and snatched a fig from a bowl of fruit. It turned to solid gold before he could take a bite. He reached out for some bread, but his fingertips had no sooner brushed against the loaf than it, too, turned to gold. He tried cheese and even a spoonful of jam, but all to no avail. "How am I to eat?" he grumbled.

"What's wrong, Father?" asked Aurelia.

"Nothing," he answered, wishing not to worry her. "Nothing at all, my child."

But Midas began to wring his hands. If he was hungry now, he imagined how much more hungry he would be by dinner. And then he began to wonder: Will I ever eat again?

Aurelia, who had been anxiously watching her father all this time, slipped out of her chair and went to comfort him. "Please don't cry," she said. Midas smiled and took her hand in his. But suddenly he recoiled in horror.

His daughter stood before him, an expression of concern frozen on her face, a teardrop clinging to her golden cheek. His cursed touch had turned Aurelia into a lifeless statue.

Midas howled in anguish and tore at his hair. He couldn't bear to look at the statue, but neither could he bear to leave her side.

ell, King Midas, are you not the happiest of men?"

Midas wiped his eyes and saw the mysterious stranger standing before him once again.

"Oh, no, I am the most miserable of men!" he cried.

"What? Did I not grant your wish for the golden touch?"

"Yes, but it is a curse to me now." Midas wept. "All that I truly loved is now lost to me."

"Do you mean to say," asked the young man, "that you would prefer a crust of bread or a cup of water to the gift of the golden touch?"

"Oh, yes!" Midas exclaimed. "I would give up all the gold in the world if only my daughter were restored to me."

"Then make your way to the river that flows past the borders of your kingdom. Follow the river upstream until you reach its source. As you cleanse yourself in the foaming spring, the golden touch will be washed away. Take with you a vase so that you may sprinkle water over any object you wish to change back to its original form." With those words, the young man vanished.

As soon as Midas reached the spring, he plunged in without removing even his shoes. As the water washed the gold from his clothes, he noticed a pretty little violet growing wild along the banks and gently brushed his finger against it. When he saw that the delicate purple flower continued to bend with the breeze, he was overjoyed.

Midas made his way back to the palace, where the first thing he did was to sprinkle the water over his beloved Aurelia. No sooner did the water touch her cheek than she was restored, laughing at her father's game and remembering not a moment of being a golden statue.

Together, the two went out to the rose garden. Midas sprinkled each frozen rose with a little river water, and Aurelia clapped her hands when she saw them cured of their golden blight.

oyfully, then, Midas restored all else he had transformed—except for a single rose, kept forever as a reminder of the golden touch.

ILLUSTRATOR'S NOTE

While the author looked to Nathaniel Hawthorne's retelling of the ancient Greek myth for inspiration, the illustrator has been influenced by other sources. "According to some scholars, the Phrygian King Midas on whom our present-day version of the myth may have been based appears to have lived in the eighth century B.C. A burial site thought to be his was found in Anatolia (now Turkey). Geometric motifs taken from artifacts discovered in the archaeological dig were incorporated into some of the scenes in this book. I chose to set the main stage for my paintings somewhere in the Middle Ages, though, to bring the tale just a bit closer to our own century. I feel that, throughout time, each generation has a person with a 'golden touch' who learns the same lesson Midas did."

For David

K.Y.C.

Oil over watercolor
was used for the full-color illustrations.
The text type is 14-point
Adobe Bernhard Modern, with 10-point leading.

Text copyright © 1999 by Charlotte Craft
Illustrations copyright © 1999 by Kinuko Y. Craft
Book design by Mahlon F. Craft

Manufactured in China by
South China Printing Company Ltd.
For information address
HarperCollins Children's Books,
a division of HarperCollins
Publishers, 195 Broadway,
New York, NY 10007.

Library of Congress Cataloging-in-Publication Data
Craft, Charlotte.
King Midas and the golden touch / as told by
Charlotte Craft ; illustrated by K. Y. Craft.
p.   cm.
Summary: A king finds himself bitterly regret-
ting the consequences of his wish that everything
he touches would turn to gold.
ISBN 0-688-13165-4
ISBN 0-688-13166-2 (lib. bdg.)
ISBN 0-06-054063-X (pbk.)
1. Midas (Legendary character)—Legends.
[1. Midas (Legendary character). 2. Mythology,
Greek.] I. Craft, Kinuko, ill. II. Title.
BL820.M55C73 1999   98-24035
398.2'0938'02—dc21   CIP
                                                  AC

14 15 16 SCP 13 12 11

❖

Visit us on the World Wide Web!
www.harperchildrens.com